Santa Claus

Has Lost His Drawers

A STORYQUEST BOOK BY

BECCI MURRAY

For Emily Campbell
StoryQuest Adventurer Extraordinaire

CHOOSE THE PAGE - UNLOCK THE ADVENTURE

ISBN: 978-1-913944-02-5

Published by Llama House Children's Books

Welcome to your StoryQuest challenge, the book where YOU are in charnge of what happens and YOU are the star of the adventure.

Start your quest on the first page, where your challenge will be explained. At the end of each chapter you'll find two options – choose a page to decide what you want to do next.

As a bonus feature, every StoryQuest book has a SPECIAL CHARACTER hidden amongst the pages. Find the character, and they'll give you a STORYQUEST STAR. This will help you unlock the ultimate ending to your adventure.

There are SO many different paths and SO many different endings – some are good, some are bad, some are happy, some are sad. Which will you choose? Will you complete the challenge? And where will your story end?

Good luck, intrepid StoryQuester, and happy reading!

A gazzilion years ago, in a time when fish had just started to grow legs, your dad made a snow-globe at school.

It has a jam-jar for a dome, a paperclip fir-tree, a plasticine hamster (could be a reindeer) and a cottonwool snowman that floats around with the glitter. Dad puts it on the mantlepiece at Christmastime, instead of putting it in the bin where it belongs, and Mum tries to sneak it into the recycling when he's not looking.

One Christmas Eve, you're turning the globe in your hands when a tiny woman pops up from behind the hamster's matchstick antlers and presses her hand against the clear surface of the globe.

Yikes! Where did *she* come from?

Curiously, you place a finger on the opposite side of the glass and – ZING! – find yourself standing in front of the woman, up to your ankles in snow.

"Thank Santa's beard you're here!" she cries. "Something terrible has happened! Something awful! It's worse than the time I accidentally gift-wrapped the

1

cat!"

You're about to ask how anyone can accidentally gift-wrap a cat, when you realise there are more important questions to be asked.

You gaze around at the vast and snowy landscape.

"Sorry, but…are we *inside* my Dad's snow-globe?"

"Thankfully, no," she replies. "I just used the globe to bring you here to the North Pole, along with a little magic of course. I'm Mrs Claus, Santa's wife, and this is our grotto." She signals to a brightly lit wooden building behind her. "I expect you're wondering what could possibly be worse than wrapping young Tiddles in sparkly paper and sticking a postage stamp on his head."

Crikey, she *posted* the poor cat too!

"Well, there's no easy way to tell you this," the woman goes on, "so I'll just come right out and say it." She takes a deep breath to steady her nerves. "SANTA CLAUS HAS LOST HIS DRAWERS!"

You frown.

"What, you mean like his cupboard drawers?"

"No, I mean like his *drawers* drawers," she says. Mrs Claus lowers her voice. "His underpants."

"UNDERPANTS?!" you cry, and a flock of arctic-pigeons takes flight from the snowy garden of the

2

grotto. "What's so terrible about that? Surely he has more than one pair of pants."

"Of course," she says, now looking a little embarrassed. "But haven't you ever wondered how Santa can visit so many houses in a single night? Well, it's all down to his lucky underpants. Without them, he'll never get all the presents delivered in time for Christmas morning."

"That's terrible," you reply. "But who would want to steal someone's underwear?"

"Oh, nobody stole them," she says. "You see, what with today being Christmas Eve and all, I washed Santa's lucky drawers and hung them out on the washing line to dry. But when I went to fetch them in again, the North Wind had blown them away. Look, there they are, flying around over the top of Craggy Mountain."

Mrs Claus points to a snowy peak, where a pair of red and green underpants is dancing around on the breeze like a rather peculiar-looking kite.

"I don't want to worry Santa so close to delivery time," says Mrs Claus, "so I've come up with a genius plan. *I'm* going to stay here and tell Santa his lucky drawers are in the tumble-drier, and *you're* going to fetch them in again."

You laugh nervously.

"You want me to trek through the sub-zero temperatures of the North Pole for an old pair of underpants?"

"You won't be alone, if that's what you're worried about." That *wasn't* what you were worried about. Well, that wasn't *all* you were worried about in any case. "I've arranged for some arctic experts to help with your quest. They're waiting for you at the bottom of Craggy Mountain. Oh, and I borrowed a couple of items from Santa's toy shed too."

Mrs Claus passes you a tennis racket and a pogo-stick. What on earth are you meant to do with a tennis racket and a pogo-stick in the middle of the North Pole?

"That's...kind," you say. "Thank you."

The woman's eyes grow wide.

"Well?" she smiles. "What do you say – will you do it?"

"I haven't got a coat," you say, "and these shoes are actually my slippers..." You see the hope on her face and sigh heavily. "But I suppose if no-one else can do it, I'll give it a go."

"That's the spirit!" hoots Mrs Claus, with a joyful clap of her hands. "Good for you! Remember, use your arctic experts wisely and don't let Santa's drawers get too far ahead. When you've caught up with them, bring them back here and your quest will be over. Now, if you'll excuse me, there's a pot of tea inside with my name on it," and as Mrs Claus goes back to her cosy grotto, you trek out across the snowy plains of the North Pole on a quest to save Santa's underpants.

Your StoryQuest has begun! Turn to page 41 to start your adventure.

Betty carries the chocolate turnip to the packing area and places it at the end of a long line of Santas. She notices another worker packing candy-canes into a box.

"Joel?" she says. The warty mountain troll turns to look at her. "Joel, is that you?"

The creature gazes up at Betty's big, hairy face and gasps.

"Betty!" he cries. "Oh, how I've missed you!"

"And I you!" sings Betty, affectionately picking him up by the ears. "That morning you got lost in the snow was the worst day of my life, but now you've come back to me and I'm never letting you go ever again!"

"Ditto, oh fuzzy-wuzzy love of my life!" exclaims Joel. "Ditto!"

Betty the Yeti has been reunited with her long-lost love. She has no intention of going anywhere without him and Joel doesn't finish work until 5:30pm, by which time Santa's drawers will be long gone.

It's true what they say – love really does make the

world go round. But sadly it won't find your underpants.

Go back to the start of the book to try again, or turn to page 45 to make a different choice.

Constructing a living yeti ladder is a piece of cake.

First, Betty slides into the crevasse and stands on Karen's shoulders. Then Hetty follows her in and stands on the shoulders of Betty. Then Letty joins the tower and you climb up the hairy ladder to free yourself from the crevasse.

Ta da!

Letty heaves her sisters up to the surface like she's pulling the plug from a bath. She does it with such skill and agility that everyone agrees *she* should be the yeti to carry you from now on.

Before long, an ice-castle appears in the distance. It has four grand turrets, a drawbridge resting over a frozen moat and a row of narrow snow-laced windows lining the top of the keep.

You watch Santa's lucky drawers fly over the building and get caught on one of the flag-poles. You'll have to go inside the castle if you want to reach them, so you head towards the —

BOOF!

Wait. What was that?

8

BOOF!

A warm Christmas pudding just hit you on the head.

BOOF!

Where are they coming from?

BOOF!

Someone inside the castle is firing them out of a cannon.

BOOF! BOOF! BOOF! BOOF!

Christmas Pudding attack! Argh!

What are you going to do?

I'll use the tennis racket to hit the puddings back where they came from. Turn to page 78.

I'll wave Karen's white scarf to surrender. Turn to page 72.

"We're chocolate Santa carvers," you tell the elf supervisor. "Yep, carving chocolate Santas is what we do best."

"Excellent," smiles Eliza Von Schweizer the Elf Supervisor, "follow me." She leads you across the factory to a huge block of chocolate. Yummy! "Carve the outside first, then hollow out the middle," she says. "I'll be round in a while to inspect it."

Carving chocolate is much harder than it looks. For one thing, it melts very easily. And for another, the temptation to eat it is almost unbearable. But you and the Yeti Sisters work fast and before long you're standing back to admire your handiwork.

Yikes! That's not a chocolate Santa – that's a chocolate turnip!

The elf supervisor spots the monstrosity from the other side of the factory.

"Blimey!" she says. "What on earth is *that* meant to be?"

You think fast and come up with two possible answers to that question. 1) You could tell her it's some kind of modern art, or, 2) You could blame it on one of the elves.

Which will you choose?

To tell the elf supervisor it's modern art, turn to page 45.

To blame the chocolate turnip on one of the elves, turn to page 37.

As the bubble-gum boulder rolls closer, you snatch one of the torches down from the wall and hold it out in front of you.

The flame is tiny. You won't be able to melt such an enormous ball with something so small. In fact, now you come to think of it, you're not sure you'll be able to melt bubble-gum with *anything*.

But the moment you pull the torch, there's a – CLICK! – and a secret doorway opens up in the side of the tunnel. You've found the switch to a hidden room!

Hurrah!

"Quickly, everyone!" you shout. "Get inside!" and you leap from the bubble-gum boulder's path in the nick of time.

Well, *that* was odd. What kind of a place has bubble-gum protecting its corridors?

As the giant ball trundles on through the passageway, you replace the torch and move deeper into the mountain. In a short while, the tunnel ends at a small, wooden door. There's an old elf standing next to it. She's wearing a red boiler suit and a green hardhat.

"What're you lot doin' 'ere?" she asks. "Don't you know it's elves only inside this 'ere mountain?"

"We, erm, *are* elves," you lie.

The elf eyes the enormous yetis. Karen's trying to untangle her hair from a rock on the ceiling.

"You're havin' a laugh, ain't cha?" snorts the elf. "You four are too big and you're obviously a human – I can tell by your tiny ears. I've worked in this mountain for almost two-'undred years and I'll bet my bottom dollar you ain't elves, or my name ain't Eliza Von Schweizer the Elf Supervisor."

"Your name is…Eliza Von Schweizer the Elf Supervisor?" you frown.

"Yes," the supervisor replies, "and if you can't prove you're elves, you'd better tell me the secret password or I ain't lettin' you through this door."

Karen starts wriggling around like she's going to wet herself.

"Oo, oo! I know it! I know it!" she cries. "I know the password!"

"Shush, Karen," hisses Letty. "You can't possibly know the password. We've never even been in this tunnel."

Will you trust Karen to say the password, or tell

Eliza Von Schweizer the truth and hope she takes pity on you?

I'll trust Karen and ask her to say the password. Turn to page 26.

I'll tell Eliza Von Schweizer the truth. Turn to page 59.

"Karen, please can you talk to the snow-fairies and tell them why we really need those drawers back?" you ask.

"I sure can," smiles Karen. She clears her throat. "Meep mee-mee mee meep-meep, mee meep-mee mee-mee meep."

The snow-fairies immediately stop fighting over the underpants.

"Mee meep-meep mee mee-meep," says the twinkliest one, "meep mee-mee meep," and Karen nods in reply.

Well, who would've believed it?

Karen really *does* know how to speak Fairy!

The tiny creature turns into a sparkling light. She flutters up to your shoulder and hands you the lucky drawers, as the rest of the flock swarm around you like fireflies.

"What's happening?!" you cry, as your feet lift up off the ground. "What are they doing to me?!"

"Don't worry," replies Karen. "They're taking you back to the grotto. I thought flying would be the quickest way for you to get there now you have Santa's drawers."

"Karen," gasps Betty, "I think that might be the first good idea you've ever had."

"Really?" she scowls. "What about the time I made Brussel sprout ice-cream? Oo, I *love* Brussel sprout ice-cream!" She thinks for a moment. "No, wait, actually, I don't."

You wave goodbye to the Yeti Sisters as the flock of snow-fairies carries you over the Frozen Ocean, past King Paulus's ice-castle, around the side of Craggy Mountain and back to the grotto. They place you down on the doorstep like a pint of milk before flying away in search of some less important clothes to steal for their nests.

Mrs Claus sees you through the window.

She flings open the front door and runs out to greet you.

"Well, bless my yule logs!" she cries. "You've only gone and done it! You've only gone and found Santa's lucky drawers! It's the most marvellous news I've had since Tiddles was stamped with RETURN TO SENDER by the Post Office and brought back here to the grotto.

"Tell me, my friend, did you find the StoryQuest

16

Star on your travels too?"

If you were given a StoryQuest Star by Neva the Ice Dragon, turn to the page number you saw glistening on it when she handed it over.
If you didn't find the StoryQuest Star, that's awesome too! Turn to page 89.

Noel the Troll watches helplessly, as the crate plummets down the slippery slope and smashes at the foot of the mountain in an explosion of chocolate.

He's furious. He takes a buffalo horn out of his jacket pocket and blows down the end of it.

TOOOOOT!

The ground starts to shake.

At first you think it's an earthquake, but then little mounds of rock start bursting up out of the snow as a hoard of trolls explodes out of the mountain. They take hold of you and the Yeti Sisters by the arms and march you off to a secret sweet factory in the middle of Craggy Mountain.

"You can stay 'ere until Christmas is over," says Noel, as a thousand elf-workers mutter and stare, "so you can't do no more damage to the festive sweets we make 'ere in the factory. Now, go and make yourselves useful and paint some jelly beans or somethin'."

Never mind, StoryQuester – you can always go back and make a different choice to continue your quest.

Go back to the start of the book to try again, or turn to page 49 to make a different choice.

Hetty picks up the chocolate turnip.

"Hey, look," she whispers, "the wooden crates are close to the exit and we need to get out of here before Santa's drawers blow too far away. Let's sneak out while nobody's looking."

The rest of you follow close behind as Hetty crosses the factory and once the turnip has been loaded into the crate, you slip through the doorway unnoticed.

You've made it to the other side of Craggy Mountain!

Awesome!

As Santa's lucky drawers move steadily away from the factory, you try your best to keep up. But the snow here is deep. *Really* deep. It's difficult to walk without sinking.

"A yeti's feet are big like skis," notes Letty. "I can carry you over the snow, if you like."

"Or *I* could carry you," offers Karen. "After all, my feet are the biggest. Plus, I *love* snow, I *love* feet and I *love* carrying people."

Which Yeti Sister will you choose to carry you over

the snow?

I'll ask Letty to carry me. Turn to page 87.
I'd like Karen to do it please. Turn to page 66.

"I'm not giving you this tennis racket," you say to Jack Frost. "I don't see why I should give you *anything* after you've just pelted us with ice-cubes."

The wicked sprite narrows his eyes. His white hair bristles and the frosty wind swirls faster around his wiry body. He breathes an icy breath into the air. It moves towards you, lifting you up like a leaf and spinning you around like a sock in a washing machine, before carrying you back across the North Pole, over the ocean and all the way home to your living-room, where Santa's lucky underpants feel like nothing more than a very strange dream.

Go back to the start of the book to try again, or turn to page 63 to make a different choice.

You decide to avoid the Frozen Ocean and walk around the ice instead. It's a really long walk and a few miles later you're starting to think you've made the wrong choice, when a set of footprints appears in the snow.

You follow the prints to a pack of dog-like creatures. They're wearing berets and chiselling a big block of ice.

"Who are they?" you ask the Yeti Sisters.

"They're arctic wolves," replies Betty. "And look, they're sculpting ice. Let's go over and take a look at their work."

Nervously, you move closer to the wolves. They're using their sharp claws to carve a polar bear into the ice.

"Why, hello," grins one of the wolves. Her yellow eyes fix on your face. "My, my, what wonderful features you have, my dear. I'm Barbara-Ruth the Arctic Wolf." Okay, so it's not the best rhyme ever, but at least her parents gave it a go. "How would you like to be the subject of my next work of art?"

23

The wolf wants to carve a sculpture of you.

Will you let her, or would you rather carry on with your quest?

I'll let her – if I don't, she might eat me. Turn to page 53.

Ice sculptures take ages – I'll carry on with my quest. Turn to page 71.

"Karen," you say, "do you think your nails are strong enough to climb out of here with me on your back?"

"I sure do!" whoops the yeti. "Jump on and let's get going!"

Karen digs her sharpened claws into the ice and scales the wall like an insect with you clinging onto her back. The higher she climbs, the scarier it gets, but soon the pair of you are climbing out and onto the snow.

"Great work, Karen," you say, getting down from the yeti's back. "Now, let's get on with our— Oh."

The other Yeti Sisters are on the opposite side of the hole. There's a gap as long as a whale between you and them. Karen has climbed up the *wrong side of the crevasse* and you can't continue your quest without a full set of arctic experts.

Sigh. Better luck next time, StoryQuester.

Go back to the start of the book to try again, or turn to page 66 to make a different choice.

"If Karen says she knows what it is, I think we should trust her," you say. "Go ahead, Karen – tell Eliza Von Schweizer the password."

The Yeti Sister puffs herself up with importance, leans down over the elf and shouts, "BIG-EARS!" right in her face.

Oh, dear.

"Karen, that's our WIFI password," sighs Betty. "And it's not 'Big-*ears*', it's 'Big-*foot*'. You know, like Uncle Abominable."

The elf looks furious. She stands on a rock to look Karen square in the eye.

"Who are you calling Big-Ears?" she snaps, pulling her hat down over her lobes.

"Oh, she didn't mean *you*," you try to explain. "She meant—"

"I know what she meant!" cries the elf. "Now get out of this mountain and don't come back! *All* of you!"

"But—"

"*OUT!*"

By the time you've walked back down the tunnel

and into the snow, Santa's drawers have blown too far away to keep up with.

To find out what's behind the door in the mountain tunnel, go back and make a different choice.

Go back to the start of the book to try again, or turn to page 12 to make a different choice.

Near the yeti cave, there's a small hole in the rock. It's the entrance to a dark tunnel, one that goes right through to the other side of the mountain and one the Yeti Sisters have not dared venture into until now.

As you duck under the low entrance, you're greeted by a row of fiery torches lining the walls of the passage. Cobwebs catch on your hair and the firelight casts eerie shadows over the floor, but you keep moving until a low rumble rattles the walls of the tunnel.

"What's that noise?" whispers Hetty, as the sound grows steadily louder.

"I don't know," replies Letty.

"Me neither," says Betty.

"It could be an elephant," suggests Karen. "Oo, I *love* elephants!"

Suddenly, an enormous boulder tumbles into view. It's pink, it's sticky and it smells like—

"BUBBLE-GUM!" yells Hetty. "IT'S A BUBBLE-GUM BOULDER AND IT'S GOING TO FLATTEN THE LOT OF US!"

28

How are you going to avoid being squashed by the boulder?

I'll use the pogo-stick to jump over it. Turn to page 76.

I'll melt the bubble-gum boulder with one of the fiery torches. Turn to page 12.

Bouncing up and down on a pogo-stick is a whole lot of fun.

Higher and higher you jump, as the yetis cheer you on from the courtyard, and soon you're leaping around like a mutant flea.

But your bouncing is out of control. You're trying to reach the top of the turret, but someone has left a window open on the second floor and suddenly you're soaring through it and—

DOOF!

You land on something soft.

It feels like a large beanbag or an enormous beachball, but looking down you see a fat walrus in a crown staring back at you.

"Kindly remove yourself from my royal blubber," he sniffs, pushing you off with a wet flipper.

"Sorry, Mr Walrus," you reply, scrambling to your feet, "I was just—"

"And please address me by my proper title. My name is King Paulus the Walrus. Now, what are you doing in my ice-castle?'"

30

At that moment, the Yeti Sisters appear at the top of a spiral staircase. What a shame you didn't notice those steps before you pogoed onto the king!

"Your Royal Tuskiness," warbles Letty with a low bow, "what an honour it is to meet such a handsome ruler. Your eyes are sparkly like jewels."

"Your moustache is fluffy like cotton-candy," adds Betty.

"Your tusks are shiny like pearls," says Hetty.

"And your stomach is round and wobbly like a big round wobbly thing," smiles Karen.

"Why, thank you," replies King Paulus, blushing. "I *am* rather proud of my wobbly tummy."

Letty winks. The yetis are distracting the king so you can sneak off and find Santa's drawers. But if you're caught wandering around the castle without the king's permission, you could be thrown into the dungeons. What do you want to do?

King Paulus looks like a reasonable walrus. I'll explain my quest and tell him about Santa's underpants. Turn to page 68.

I'll take my chances with the dungeons and sneak off. Turn to page 91.

"You found it!" cries Mrs Claus, as you hand her the StoryQuest Star. "You've unlocked the ultimate end to your story! Now, close your eyes and count to ten – I have a surprise for you."

When you reopen your eyes, you find yourself back in your living-room. Dad's snow-globe is still on the mantlepiece and Mrs Claus is waving goodbye from inside. If only you'd had chance to say a proper farewell to the Yeti Sisters too.

"Oo, I love magic snow-globes," says a familiar voice from behind you.

You turn to find Karen perched on the edge of your windowsill and the other three yetis sitting right there on your sofa.

"What are you all doing here?" you gasp.

"Mrs Claus sent us," replies Betty. "Our quest is to make sure you have the best Christmas ever, as a thank you for all your hard work. We're going to make *loads* of icy treats."

"Like snow-cones and slushies," says Hetty.

"Arctic rolls and ice-lollies," adds Letty.

"Raspberry sorbet and chocolate ice-cream," says Betty.

"And baked beans on toast," smiles Karen.

"But before we start the festivities," Betty goes on, "why don't you give that snow-globe a shake?"

Confused, you pick up the jam-jar and turn it over in your hands. You watch as the glitter swirls gently inside, until suddenly, looking out through your living room window, you realise it's starting to snow.

"It's going to be a white Christmas!" you cheer. "What a wonderful surprise!"

Karen presses her nose against the windowpane.

"I love snow," she sighs, blissfully. "But the thing I love *most*, is a happy ending."

Congratulations! You've completed your challenge and found the StoryQuest Star – you're an awesome arctic adventurer! Take a look in the back of this book for more StoryQuest challenges.

"Somebody stop that crate!" you cry, and the Yeti Sisters immediately jump into action.

"Don't worry!" shouts Betty

"We've got this!" cries Hetty.

"We'll stop it!" yells Letty.

"Weeeeeee!" squeals Karen, as she slides down the side of the mountain.

You've never seen such fantastic skiing skills. The yetis wind down the slope, darting between the rocks, sliding in and out of the trees, until all four of them are in front of the crate.

SCREEEEECH!

They stop the wooden box with their big, furry hands just before it reaches the bottom of the mountain.

Phew!

"Your yetis have saved my chocolate Santas," smiles the troll, as you head back down the slope you just climbed. "In return for your kindness, let me offer you some free advice – if you want to get to the other side of this rock, you should use the mountain tunnel instead of climbing that peak again. There's an elf guarding a door at the far end of the passage. Tell her I sent you and she'll let you through," and with that, Noel the Troll heads off towards the grotto.

Near the yeti cave, there's a small hole in the rock. It's the entrance to a dark tunnel, one that goes right through to the other side of the mountain and one the Yeti Sisters have not dared venture into until now.

As you duck under the low entrance, you're greeted by a row of fiery torches lining the walls of the passage. Cobwebs catch on your hair and the firelight casts eerie shadows over the floor, but you keep moving until a low rumble rattles the walls of the tunnel.

"What's that noise?" whispers Hetty, as the sound grows steadily louder.

"I don't know," replies Letty.

"Me neither," says Betty.

"It could be an elephant," suggests Karen. "Oo, I *love* elephants!"

Suddenly, an enormous boulder tumbles into view. It's pink, it's sticky and it smells like—

"BUBBLE-GUM!" yells Hetty. "IT'S A BUBBLE-GUM BOULDER AND IT'S GOING TO FLATTEN THE LOT OF US!"

Cripes, StoryQuester, you'll have to think fast!

What are you going to do to avoid being squashed by the bubble-gum boulder?

To use the pogo-stick to jump over the bubble-gum boulder, turn to page 51.
To melt the bubble-gum with one of the torches, turn to page 80.

"It wasn't *us* who carved that giant turnip," you tell the elf supervisor. "It was, erm...*him!*"

You point at one of the elves, who looks quizzically back at you.

He just carved an intricate reindeer out of white chocolate. You can literally see every hair on the creature's body.

"So, what you're telling me," begins Eliza Von Schweizer the Elf Supervisor, "is our most experienced chocolate carver, one who has worked in this department for almost three-hundred years and one who also happens to be *my brother* by the way, is responsible for carving this poor example of a root vegetable instead of a Santa."

"Well," you reply, sheepishly, "when you put it like that, it does sound a bit far-fetched."

Eliza Von Schweizer is unimpressed with your carving skills and sends you to the Training Department to perfect your craft.

It takes five years to become a qualified chocolatier and Santa's drawers will have reached the *South* Pole by the time you've finished.

Go back to the start of the book to try again, or turn to page 10 to make a different choice.

If you learnt anything from fairy tales, it's *never trust a wolf*, so you leave the pack to their ice-sculpting and continue around the edge of the Frozen Ocean.

You walk and you walk for what feels like forever, as the temperature drops with every step. Even the yetis are cold and soon the air becomes thick with snow. It's difficult to see through the downpour of white and Santa's drawers vanish into the haze.

You're lost in an arctic blizzard and have to wait until someone comes out to rescue you, but at least you have four hairy yetis to huddle up with in the meantime.

Go back to the start of the book to try again, or turn to page 71 to make a different choice.

When you step into the icy lift, you realise it wasn't built with four yetis and a human in mind. It's like trying to squeeze a family of cats into a matchbox.

You close the door and press the 'up' button. The whole elevator makes a terrible creaking noise, like an old rope trying to lift a steam-train, and then—

CLONK!

It stops.

Oh no, you're stuck in a lift with your nose pressed into Karen's left armpit (yuck!) and you'll have to wait for an engineer to come out and fix it. Of course, you don't get many lift engineers in the North Pole, because, well, you don't get many lifts in the North Pole, so the toy soldiers have to fly someone over from Sweden to rescue you. By the time the engineer arrives, Christmas is long gone and so are your chances of finishing this quest.

Go back to the start of the book to try again, or turn to page 72 to make a different choice.

You trudge through the thick snow until reaching the foot of Craggy Mountain. There's a small cave in front of you, but your arctic experts are nowhere in sight.

"Hello?" you call out, your breath clouding in the cold air. "Is anyone home?"

A pair of yellow eyes shines through the darkness. A hairy foot appears, followed by a hairy ankle and a hairy leg, before a hairy body steps out of the hole and you find yourself face to face with a big, hairy yeti.

She's grinning from ear to ear and she's covered from head to toe in (you guessed it) hair.

"Wotcha," smiles the yeti. "You must be the StoryQuester Mrs Claus told us about. I'm Betty the Yeti and these are my sisters – Hetty, Letty and Karen."

Three more yetis walk out of the cave.

"You're a *human!*" cheers Karen. She's wearing a little white scarf, despite being woollier than even the woolliest mammoth. "Oo, I *love* humans!"

Karen picks something green out of her fangs, inspects it for a moment and then pops it back into her mouth.

"Now, we need to catch Santa's lucky drawers before the end of the day," explains Letty, pointing up at the red and green underpants still twirling around over the peak of Craggy Mountain. "They're not moving too fast, but we'll still need to get to the other side of the mountain if we want to catch up with them."

"We could climb over the top of it," suggests Hetty.

"Or we could go through the mountain tunnel," offers Betty.

Okay, StoryQuester, it's time to make your first choice. Which yeti's advice will you follow?

I'll do as Hetty suggests and climb over the top of Craggy Mountain. Turn to page 92.
I'll do as Betty suggests and go through the mountain tunnel. Turn to page 28.

"I have an idea," you say to the yetis. "How about one of you roars at the robins to scare some of them away?"

"That's an excellent idea," replies Betty. "It would be my pleasure."

"Erm, I think you mean it would be *my* pleasure," says Hetty. "After all, *I'm* the one with the biggest mouth."

"But *my* roar is the scariest," says Letty. "The only thing scarier than *my* roar is Karen's collection of ear-wax dinosaurs."

"Oo, I *love* ear-wax dinosaurs!" cries Karen.

Which yeti would you like to—

"*ROOOOAAAAAARRRRR!*"

Oh. Too late.

The three yetis have all roared at once and the flock of birds are terrified. They let go of their ribbons and zip away into the sky, as the wooden crate plummets towards the snowy peak of Craggy Mountain.

There's a troll from the factory below you. He's pulling a crate towards the grotto. But when four yetis and a human land on his foot, he lets go of the box, clutches his leg and the crate slides away down the side of the mountain.

The troll is furious. He takes a buffalo horn out of his jacket pocket and blows down the end of it.

TOOOOOT!

The ground starts to shake. At first you think it's an earthquake, but then little mounds of rock start bursting up out of the snow and a hoard of trolls explodes from the peak of the mountain. They seize hold of you and the Yeti Sisters, before marching you back to the factory.

"You can stay 'ere until Christmas is over," says the troll, as the elves all mutter and stare, "so you can't do no more damage to the festive sweets we make 'ere in the factory."

"But I have to find Santa's underpants!" you cry.

"Yeah, yeah," scoffs the troll, "and I have to look for the tooth-fairy's knickers. Now, make yourself useful and paint some candy-canes."

Go back to the start of the book to try again, or turn to page 46 to make a different choice.

"It's modern art," you tell the stunned elf. "Don't you like it?"

Eliza Von Schweizer frowns. She takes a step back from the eyesore you just called 'art' and tilts her head.

"Hmm," she muses, "you've captured the profoundness of the Christmas season in an abstract interpretation of a traditional subject. I like it."

You have no idea what she just said.

"Erm, thanks," you reply. "What shall we do with it now?"

"Oh, just bung it over there with the others," she replies.

The elf supervisor points to a line of wooden crates. A group of mountain trolls are loading them up with goodies, but when you try to pick up the chocolate turnip, you find it's too heavy to lift. You'll have to choose a yeti to carry it instead. Who will you trust with this delicate job?

☆

To choose Hetty, turn to page 20.

To choose Betty, turn to page 6.

Disguising a seven-foot yeti as a jelly bean is far from easy. But your painting skills are good and soon all five of you are diving into the crate of sweets, where you blend in like a fart in a sewer.

You feel the box being wheeled to the exit and out of the mountain. When the movement stops, you peep through the jelly beans. A flock of robins is fluttering over the crate. They're tying Christmas ribbons to the corners and lifting the box into the air, along with yourself and all four of the yetis.

Santa's lucky drawers are travelling west and the robins are carrying you east. You need to get out of this crate before you lose sight of the underpants.

I'll ask one of the Yeti Sisters to roar at the robins and scare some of them away. Turn to page 43.
I'll jump out of the crate. Turn to page 77.

"Brrrrilliant!" cries Jack Frost, as you hand him the tennis racket. "And in return for this splendid gift, I'll tell you a secret about Santa's drawers. It wasn't a *wind* that took them – they were stolen by *snow-fairies!*"

Betty scowls.

"Pull the other one," she says. "It's got reindeer bells on it."

"It's true," he insists. "Fairies aren't the cute little imps you find in picture books, you know. They're devious critters with sharp teeth and they steal people's clothes to line their nests. They're up there right now, fighting over Santa's underpants to see who gets to keep them."

"A likely story!" snorts Hetty. "I can't see any fairies."

"That's because they're flying," says Jack, "and snow-fairies are no more than a tiny sparkle when they're in flight. If you don't believe me, I'll *show* you instead."

He turns his pale face up to the sky and breathes an icy wind at the drawers. His breath swirls into a funnel, pulling the underpants closer, and closer, and closer still, until—

BUMP!

A flock of snow-fairies tumbles onto the ground.

Blimey, Jack Frost was telling the truth!

"Meep mee-mee meep mee meep!" the fairies shout crossly, shaking their fists and baring their teeth as they fight their way out from under the pants. "Mee meep-meep mee!"

You have no idea what they're saying.

"Oo, I love snow-fairies!" cries Karen. "I can *speak* Fairy, you know. Shall I talk to them and explain why we need those drawers back?"

"That depends," says Letty. "When you say you know how to speak Fairy, is it like the time you said you knew how to play the banjo then asked if we were playing for a line or a full-house?"

Will you trust Karen to speak to the snow-fairies, or will you snatch the underpants and be on your way?

I'll let Karen to talk to the snow-fairies. Turn to page 15.

I'll snatch the underpants and be on my way. Turn to page 94.

"Quickly!" you call out to the Yeti Sisters. "Everyone take shelter behind the troll's crate!"

The wooden box makes a great wind-shield and sitting amongst four huge yetis is pretty cosy. You wait patiently in your hiding place until the wind stops and Noel the Troll turns back into flesh and bones.

"Hey, what're you doin' near my crate?" he demands. "Get away from that before you break it!"

"There's no need to be rude," replies Betty.

"We haven't caused any damage," says Hetty.

"We didn't even touch it," adds Letty.

"Yes, Noel," says Karen, "stop being such a worry-wart. It's as good as new, see?" and she taps the side of the crate to demonstrate her point.

Of course, Karen is a yeti. Karen is a very big, very strong yeti. Saying a yeti tapped a crate is like saying a sledgehammer tapped an ant.

The big wooden box shoots down the side of Craggy Mountain like a rocket.

VROOSH!

"*Noooo!*" cries the troll. Noel watches in horror as

49

the box races towards the ground. "There are two giant chocolate Santas in there and they'll be smashed to pieces if you don't do something!"

Uh oh. What are you going to do?

I'll ask the Yeti Sisters to chase after it. Turn to page 34.

I don't have time to worry about chocolate Santas. Noel can rescue his own crate – let's get on with the quest. Turn to page 18.

A pogo-stick is perfect for bouncing over giant bubble-gum boulders. In fact, you're fairly sure it's the reason they were invented.

But you forgot about the Yeti Sisters.

When you jump over the tumbling obstacle, the yetis are still in its path and the sticky, pink ball of gum ploughs into them with a terrible *SQUELCH!* Their fur sticks to the ball and they're carried out of the mountain and across the white plains of the cold North Pole.

It's nothing to worry about – the Yetis will be fine once they finally stop rolling. But you can't finish your quest without them, so you're forced to go back to the grotto and tell Mrs Claus what happened.

Go back to the start of the book to try again, or turn to page 34 to make a different choice.

51

You dash towards the nearest wave and take cover from the flying ice-cubes.

"You have no idea how hot it is to run in all this fur," puffs Karen, as she slides in next to you. "I could really use a drink right now." Her eyes fix on the frozen wave. "Oo, ice – even better!"

Before you can stop her, Karen licks the frozen wave. Her long tongue sticks to its surface like glue.

"Oh, Karen, not again," sighs Hetty. "That's the fourth time this week."

Hetty has to travel all the way back to the cave to bring Karen a warm cup of tea. She uses it to thaw out her sister's tongue, as Santa's lucky drawers disappear into the blurry mist of the Frozen Ocean.

You're *so* close to finishing your challenge, StoryQuester! Go back to make a different choice and you'll soon have those underpants back where they belong.

Go back to the start of the book to try again, or turn to page 95 to make a different choice.

"That's very kind of you, Barbara," you say to the wolf. "I'd love it if you made an ice-sculpture of me."

"Grrreat!" she replies. "Now, stand very still – this won't take long."

Five sharp claws spring out of the wolf's hand.

GULP!

She uses them to carve a magnificent image into the ice. It's so good it could almost be your twin.

"You're incredibly talented," you say, when the sculpture is finished. "Thank you so much, Barbara. It was really nice to meet you, but we must be on our way now."

"Erm, just a minute," says the wolf. "This carving is my gift to you. You're not going to *leave* it here, are you? I'd be terribly upset if you did."

You gawp up at the enormous lump of ice.

Then you look at the wolves, who are snarling quietly through their pointed teeth.

Hurriedly, you and the Yeti Sisters pick up the sculpture. You hoist it onto your shoulders and stagger across the snow, leaving the wolves to their artwork.

But the ice is so heavy, it slows your pace to a crawl
and before long Santa's lucky drawers have blown so
far over the Frozen Ocean they're almost in Finland.

Go back to the start of the book to try again, or turn to
page 23 to make a different choice.

"A silver fairy key!" cries Neva, as you take the item out of your pocket. "Fairy keys are magical and can open any door. Give it a try and see if it works."

When you place the key into the lock, the grate crackles as the magic flows into its metal bars and with a click barrier opens.

Awesome!

Neva pulls herself out of the dungeon and onto the floor of the turret. She's a young ice-dragon, about the same size as a large horse, and she swishes her magnificent tail happily over the floor.

"I'm free!" she cheers. "Now I can be with my family on Christmas Day! I don't know how I can ever repay you, my friend, but maybe *this* will show my gratitude in some small way."

The ice-dragon tilts back her head and blows a stream of snow out of her mouth. The glistening flakes swirl in the air before forming the shape of a star.

It flutters down into the palm of your hand. There's a picture of Mrs Claus on one side and the number 32 on the other.

"A StoryQuest Star!" you exclaim. "Wow, Neva, thank you so much!"

"Memorise the number on the back of the star, then take it to Mrs Claus when you've finished your quest," smiles the dragon. "It will unlock the ultimate end to your story. Now leave this castle before King Paulus finds out you've released me and locks you away in his dungeon. Merry Christmas, my friend, and thank you," and as Neva the ice-dragon soars up into the pale sky, you head back downstairs with the StoryQuest Star tucked safely inside your pocket.

Congratulations! You've found the StoryQuest Star!

Turn to page 85 to continue your quest.

"Excuse me," you call across the factory, hopping around as if ready to wet yourself, "I really need a wee. Is it all right if I pop outside for a moment?"

"Outside?" frowns Eliza Von Schweizer. "Why would you want to do it outside? We do *have* toilets, you know."

Oh. You hadn't thought of that.

"Yes, but I'd prefer to do it outside," you say. You don't know where you're going with this, but it can't be anywhere good. "You see, I always do it outside, because I, erm, live on a farm."

"On a farm?" scowls the elf supervisor. "There's a farm in middle of the North Pole?"

"That's right. It's a penguin farm."

Eliza Von Schweizer gasps dramatically. She presses a big, red button on the side of the jelly bean machine. An alarm blares out from the heart of the mountain and before you know what's happening, the other elves are pouncing on you and the Yeti Sisters.

They tie you up with strawberry laces and the elf supervisor shines a fairy light in your face.

"Penguins are the sworn enemies of the elf community," she says, "and anyone who lives on a penguin farm, must be one of their spies. Now, human, tell us everything you know and we'll set you free."

Well, this was quite an unexpected turn of events. But at least you get to eat the strawberry laces once you're finally released.

Go back to the start of the book to try again, or turn to page 65 to make a different choice.

You explain your quest to Eliza Von Schweizer the Elf Supervisor.

"Here's the thing," you say. "I'm on a quest to find Santa's drawers and—"

"Well, I never," gasps the elf. "That's correct."

You scowl.

"What is?"

"'Santa's drawers' is the secret password, so I suppose you *must* be elves after all!" Eliza Von Schweizer tilts back her head to look up at your yeti friends. "I suppose some of us just grow faster than others." The elf takes a key from her pocket. "Anyway, welcome to the Christmas Sweet Factory."

She opens the door and a great gust of sugary air wafts out from a cavernous room carved into the rock. There are hundreds of machines, all whirring and chugging in time with the singing of a thousand elves, as an endless line of sugary treats moves from place to place on a twisting maze of conveyor belts.

A sweet factory in the middle of a mountain?

Cool!

"Now, let me give you one of these keys," says the elf supervisor, "so you can let yourselves in on your next shift. It's made by fairies, so best you take care of it." You place the key into your pocket. "Righty-o, get to work then."

"Work?" says Betty.

"That's right – why else would you be here? The only vacancies we have at the moment are in the Chocolate Santa Carvin' Department and the Jelly Bean Paintin' Team. Which job did you apply for?"

If you want the elf supervisor to believe you're an elf, you'll have to pretend to work here. Which department will you choose?

To join the Chocolate Santa Carving Department, turn to page 10.
To join the Jelly Bean Painting Team, turn to page 65.

The growling turns into a sob as you tip-toe towards the grate and peer through the metal bars.

The dungeon is dark and damp, and the dim light from the outside world casts an eerie glow on the floor. And there, within the shadows, trembling like a frightened puppy, you see the quivering shape of a—

Crikey, that's a *dragon!*

You gasp loudly and the creature's crystal white face turns to look at you.

"Please don't go," she says, gently. "I've been down here for days."

The dragon's eyes are like the ocean and her pearly skin catches the light like a jewel.

"Who are you?" you ask.

"My name is Neva. I'm an ice-dragon. The king locked me inside this dungeon so I couldn't melt his castle with my fiery breath. But I'm an *ice*-dragon. I don't breathe fire, I breathe snow. I'd be so grateful if you'd open the grate for me."

You look around the turret for something to lever it open with, but find nothing. Perhaps you could use the handle of your tennis racket. Or maybe you've collected a key on your travels.

What are you going to do?

This tennis racket must be good for something – let's lever it open. Turn to page 70.

I collected a key from Eliza Von Schweizer the Elf Supervisor – let's try that. Turn to page 55.

Using the tennis racket to bat away the ice-cubes, you walk further out onto the frozen water.

Suddenly, Jack Frost appears from behind one of the waves. His skin is blue, his hair is silver and he has a nose so sharp you could open tins with it. There's a fierce wind twirling around him like a tiny hurricane, whipping the snow into ice-cubes and hurling them over the ocean.

"Trespassers!" he shouts, in his terrible rage. "How dare you hit my ice-cubes away with your—" He stops throwing the ice and squints at the racket in your hand. "What *is* that?" he asks.

"It's a tennis racket," you tell him. "Haven't you ever seen a tennis racket before?"

"No," he replies, "and having to whip up this wind to pelt the polar bears with ice is such hard work – it would be a lot easier if I had that tennis racket to do it with instead."

"We're not here about the racket," you reply. "Jack Frost, I think *you* are responsible for the strange wind that's carrying Santa's drawers across the North Pole. I saw the pants sparkling when they were stuck on King Paulus's castle, so I know there's magic at work."

"Hm, it does *sound* like something I'd do," Jack Frost replies. "In fact, I wish I'd thought of it myself. But sadly, I am not to blame." He offers you a smug grin. "But I know who *is* responsible. Give me that tennis racket and I'll tell you everything."

Jack Frost wants your tennis racket in exchange for important information about Santa's drawers. Will you believe him and hand over the racket? Or will you tell him to take a running jump off a very short iceberg?

Okay, I'll give him the tennis racket – I need to do everything I can to save Christmas. Turn to page 47.

Give him my racket? Not on your nelly! Turn page 22.

Jelly bean painting is great fun. The Yeti Sisters are surprisingly good at it, despite having fingers like sausages and claws longer than your dad's toenails.

But you have a quest to be getting on with and you can't afford to waste too much time painting sweets – you need to get out of here as fast as you can.

Scanning the room, you locate the exit. It's at the very back of the factory, close to your machine. You could make a run for it, but there are elves everywhere. Plus, there's a hoard of trolls putting sweets into crates and hauling them out through the same door. Someone is bound to see you and if Eliza Von Schweizer finds out, she'll send you all back down the tunnel.

Dun dun duuuuh!

How will you escape from Craggy Mountain without making the elves and trolls suspicious?

I'll say I need the toilet. Turn to page 57.
I'll paint myself and the yetis bright colours and hide in a jelly-bean crate. Turn to page 46.

65

You climb onto Karen's back and the hairy yeti carries you over the snowy plain.

"I *love* snow," she says, walking merrily along in the pale morning light. "I love sunshine too of course, but I *really* love snow."

"Me too," you reply. "It doesn't snow much where I come from, so—"

"And cabbage. I love cabbage. Especially at Christmas. And chairs, yeah, I love chairs. Wooden chairs mostly, but I love the plastic ones too. Do you like peanut butter? I love it. But spaghetti hoops are my favourite, I love spaghetti hoops and grated cheese on toast..."

Karen's not concentrating on where she's going and it's difficult to see in front of her through all this yeti hair. So the first thing you know about the enormous ice crevasse is when you fall into it.

"*WHEEEEEEE!*" squeals Karen, as you slip down the ice and disappear into the ground. "I *love* slides!"

When you reach the bottom, you look up. The other three Yeti Sisters are staring down at you.

How are you going to get out of the ice crevasse?

I'll ask the Yeti Sisters to stand on each other's shoulders and form a living ladder. Turn to page 8.
Karen's claws are like talons. I'll ask her to scale the wall of ice and carry me out of the crevasse. Turn to page 25.

You're worried King Paulus will throw you into the dungeon, so instead of sneaking away you quickly explain your quest.

"Santa's drawers, eh?" nods the king. His moustache bristles. "Those are the luckiest underpants in the world, so they say."

"I know," you reply, "which is why we need to get them down from that flagpole before tonight's Christmas deliveries."

The king smiles.

"No problem. Guards, fetch Santa's drawers and bring them here immediately."

The wooden soldiers march off and retrieve the underpants. Upon their return, King Paulus the Walrus snatches them out of their hands and pulls them over his head like a hat.

"Finders keepers," he grins. "Now *I* have the luckiest pants in the world instead of that silly oaf, Santa. Guards, throw these trespassers out of my castle and raise the drawbridge."

And with that, he waddles away to admire himself

68

in a mirror.

Go back to the start of the book to try again, or turn to page 30 to make a different choice.

The handle of the tennis racket fits perfectly into the grate, so you poke it through and stand on the opposite end.

CRACK!

The grate remains shut and the racket snaps in two. A piece of it flies down the staircase. You hear a yelp as it strikes King Paulus on the end of his tusk and he storms up to the turret, angrier than a wasp at a barbecue.

An army of toy soldiers are summoned. They throw you into the dungeon with Neva for the rest of the festive season, where you celebrate Christmas by singing carols so loudly it drives King Paulus the Walrus quite potty.

Go back to the start of the book to try again, or turn to page 61 to make a different choice.

"Thanks for the offer," you say to the wolf, "but I'm on a quest to take Santa's underpants back to the grotto." You point up at the lucky drawers. "That's why we're walking around this ocean."

"The Frozen Ocean surrounds the whole of the Northern Hemisphere," replies Barbara-Ruth the Arctic Wolf. "If you keep walking, you'll just go around in circles. You'll need to go *on* the ice if you want to reach those underpants."

"But it looks too slippery for me to walk on," you say.

The wolf smiles. Her teeth are so shiny you can see your reflection in them.

"Then let me help you," she grins.

Will you accept the wolf's help? Or will you continue to walk around the Frozen Ocean?

I'll accept the wolf's help. Turn to page 83.
I'd like to keep walking around the Frozen Ocean. Turn to page 39.

"Quick, Karen, pass me your scarf!" you cry, and you take the makeshift flag and wave it over your head.

The Christmas pudding attack stops immediately and a group of wooden soldiers runs out from the castle. Their knees are knocking together like two empty coconut shells.

"*Wood* you look at that snuggly scarf!" cries one of them.

"I *wood*!" cheers another.

"So *wood* I!" says a third.

"I don't suppose you *wood* let us borrow it if we promise to let you inside? The castle is freezing and we can't turn the heating on or the whole place *wood* melt. That scarf *wood* warm us up no end."

"Oo, I love toy soldiers!" cries Karen. "Here, take the scarf – it's yours!"

"Thank you, thank you!" cheers the soldier. "It *wood* usually be our job to pummel you with Christmas puddings if you tried to enter these walls, but we *wood* do no such thing now you've given us such a fine gift. Welcome to the castle of King Paulus VI."

Thanking the soldiers, you cross the moat and enter the castle grounds. From the courtyard, you see Santa's drawers still stuck on the end of a flagpole at the top of a turret.

"Look, an ice-elevator," says Hetty, pointing to a frosted door in the back wall of the castle. "We could use that to get up to the underpants."

"Or you could use the pogo-stick to bounce your way up," suggests Betty.

Which yeti's advice *wood* you—

I mean, which yeti's advice would you like to follow?

I'll follow Hetty's advice and take the ice-elevator.
Turn to page 40.
I'll follow Betty's advice and use the pogo-stick. Turn to page 30.

"Quickly!" you call out to the Yeti Sisters. "Everyone lie on their stomachs so we don't get blown back down the mountain!"

You all lie on the very steep, very slippery mountainside, the slopes of which are difficult to stay on even *without* a gale-force wind.

Suddenly, all five of you slip down the slope like toboggans.

"*ARRRRGH!*" you shout.

"*ARRRRGH!*" cries Betty.

"*ARRRRGH!*" yells Hetty.

"*ARRRRGH!*" wails Letty.

"*WEEEEEE!*" squeals Karen, and you all crash into a heap at the foot of the mountain.

You've hurt your leg, Betty has twisted her ankle, Hetty has bumped her head, Letty has grazed her elbow and Karen is heading back up the mountain for another turn.

Feeling a bit sorry for yourself, you limp back to the grotto with your tail between your legs, where Mrs Claus sends you through the snow-globe and into the warmth of your living-room to recover.

Go back to the start of the book to try again, or turn to page 92 to make a different choice.

A pogo-stick is perfect for bouncing over giant bubble-gum boulders. In fact, you're fairly sure it's the reason they were invented.

But you forgot about the Yeti Sisters. So when you jump over the tumbling obstacle, your arctic assistants are still in its path and the sticky, pink ball of gum ploughs into them with a terrible *SQUELCH!*

The ball sticks to their fur. It carries them out of the mountain and across the North Pole, trundling over the snow like an enormous bowling ball.

Don't worry, StoryQuester – the sisters will be fine. But you can't finish your quest without them, so you'd better go back to the grotto and tell Mrs Claus what has happened.

Go back to the start of the book to try again, or turn to page 28 to make a different choice.

You jump out of the jelly-bean crate and drop towards Craggy Mountain.

Luckily, the slopes are buried under a thick layer of snow. It cushions your fall as you and the Yeti Sisters plop into the soft flakes like cherries on top of a trifle.

"Let's do it again!" cries Karen. "I *love* plummeting from obscene heights!"

Scrambling to your feet, you see Santa's underpants moving away from Craggy Mountain. You try to keep up with them, but the snow here is deep. *Really* deep. It's difficult to walk without sinking.

"A yeti's feet are big like skis," notes Letty. "I can carry you over the snow, if you like."

"Or *I* could carry you," offers Karen. "After all, my feet are the biggest."

Which Yeti Sister will you choose to carry you over the snow?

I'll ask Letty to carry me. Turn to page 87.
I'd like Karen to do it please. Turn to page 66.

Brandishing your tennis racket like a pro-player, you thwack the Christmas puddings back towards the castle.

The head of a walrus pops up on the highest turret. One of the puddings hits him right between the eyes. It explodes in a jumble of currants and cherries.

The walrus wipes his face with the back of his flipper, and, "LOAD THE CATAPULT!" he bawls.

A group of wooden soldiers wheel an enormous catapult onto the roof. They place something wobbly into the sling. You can't make out what it is, but it's roughly the size of an elephant and…is that *cream* on top of it?

"It's a giant strawberry trifle!" yells Betty. "Quick, everyone, take cover!"

The catapult flings the gigantic dessert across the wall of the castle, where it lands on top of you with a loud—

SPLAT!

The world goes dark and sticky, but it tastes fantastic. It's going to take forever to eat your way out of here and frankly you couldn't care less.

Scrummy!

Go back to the start of the book to try again, or turn to page 8 to make a different choice.

As the bubble-gum boulder rolls closer, you snatch the nearest torch from the wall and hold it out in front of you. The flame is tiny. You won't be able to melt such an enormous ball with *that* thing. And now you come to think of it, you're not sure you'll be able to melt bubble-gum with *anything*.

But the moment you pull the torch from the wall, there's a – *CLICK!* – and a secret doorway opens up in the side of the tunnel.

You've found a hidden room! Hurrah!

"Come on, everyone!" you shout. "Get inside!" and you leap out of the bubble-gum boulder's path in the nick of time.

As the giant ball trundles on through the passage, you replace the torch and move deeper into the mountain. In a short while, the tunnel ends at a small, wooden door. There's an old elf standing next to it. She's wearing a red boiler suit and a green hardhat.

"What're you lot doin' 'ere?" she asks. "Don't you know it's elves only inside this 'ere mountain? And you lot en't elves or my name en't Eliza Von Schweizer the Elf Supervisor."

"We're not elves," you reply. (Sorry, did she just say, Eliza Von Schweizer the Elf Supervisor?) "Noel the Mountain Troll sent us."

"Ah, Noel is a good friend of mine," says the elf, taking a key from her pocket. "If Noel sent you then...welcome to the Christmas Sweet Factory."

Eliza Von Schweizer opens the door and a great gust of sugary air wafts out from a cavernous room carved into the middle of the mountain. There are hundreds of machines, all whirring and chugging in time with the singing of a thousand elves, as an endless line of sweets moves from place to place on a twisting maze of conveyor belts.

"Now, let me give you one of these keys," says the elf supervisor, "so you can let yourselves in on your next shift. It's made by fairies, so best you take care of it." You put the key into your pocket. "Righty-o, get to work then."

"Work?" frowns Betty.

"Yes," replies the elf. "No-one's allowed in the factory unless they're here to work, so it's either that or I send you back where you came from. The only vacancies we have at the moment are in the Chocolate Santa Carvin' Department or the Jelly Bean Paintin'

Team. Which job are you here for?"

You'll have to pretend to work here if you want to reach the other side of this mountain. Choose your department, StoryQuester!

To join the Chocolate Santa Carving Department, turn to page 10.

If you fancy a job as a jelly bean painter, turn to page 65.

When you ask the wolf to help you, her polished smile widens.

"Super," she grins. "This won't take a jiffy."

Five needle-like claws spring out of her paw.

GULP!

She picks up a heavy chunk of ice.

GULP!

She cuts through the block like butter with a swish of her paw.

GULP!

And in a blur of wolf fur, she carves you the finest pair of ice-skates you've ever seen.

"There you go," says Barbara, finishing off the detail with the tip of her fang. "You'll have no trouble walking across the Frozen Ocean in these."

"That's amazing," you say, as you try out the skates. They fit perfectly. "Thank you!"

Waving goodbye to the wolf-pack, you skate out onto the ice with your yeti friends in pursuit of Santa's underpants. But you don't get far before an ice-cube flies in out of nowhere. It whistles past your ear, hits the frozen wave behind you and smashes like glass, as another one shoots over your head.

"It's Jack Frost!" wails Letty. "He's pummelling us with ice-cubes! I thought Christmas puddings were bad enough, but at least they were soft. What are we going to do?"

"We could make slushies with them," shrugs Karen.

You can't follow Karen's suggestion, because, well, it's a stupid one. Which means you have two choices: hit the ice-cubes back with the tennis racket, or take cover behind one of the frozen waves.

What's the plan, StoryQuester?

To take cover behind one of the waves, turn to page 90.

To hit the ice-cubes back with the tennis racket, turn to page 63.

At the bottom of the stairs you find the Yeti Sisters still flattering King Paulus the Walrus. It's lucky you came back when you did, because it sounds like they're running out of ideas.

"Your flippers are so slimy," says Betty.

"Your nostrils are so hairy," says Hetty.

"Your skin is so warty," says Letty.

"And your ears are so..." Karen stops to inspect the walrus's head. "Oh, you don't *have* any ears."

"Time to go!" you cry, interrupting their chat before it gets you all into trouble. "It was lovely to meet you, King Paulus, but we have to go now – the yetis have a hair appointment at 3 o'clock," and you wink at the four sisters.

"What's wrong with your eye?" frowns Karen.

Before long, you're crossing the moat and heading back onto the snow. Santa's underpants are gaining speed and by the time you've told the Yeti Sisters what happened on top of the turret, the drawers have drifted over a huge stretch of frozen water.

A grey mist hangs in the air like smoke.

85

"It's the Frozen Ocean," gasps Hetty. "I've read about this place in books. Jack Frost lives here. He doesn't take kindly to trespassers and those frozen waves will be tricky for a human to walk on."

Do you want to brave the Frozen Ocean, or try to avoid it instead?

To brave the Frozen Ocean, turn to page 95.
To avoid it, turn to page 23.

Choosing Letty to carry you is a great decision. In fact, Letty won a gold medal in the 100 Metre Human-Carrying Race at the Winter Olympics. She was on the front cover of Yeti Sports Weekly and everything.

As the sunlight sparkles the ground like glitter, you follow Santa's drawers across the snow until a glassy structure appears in the distance.

It's an *ice-castle!* It has four grand turrets, one at each corner, an open drawbridge resting over a frozen moat and a row of narrow snow-laced windows lining the top of the keep.

You watch Santa's lucky drawers fly over the castle and get caught on one of the flag-poles. It looks like you'll have to go inside if you want to reach them, so you—

BOOF!

Wait. What was that?

BOOF!

A warm Christmas pudding just landed on your head.

BOOF!

87

Where are they coming from?

BOOF!

Someone inside the castle is firing them out of a cannon.

BOOF! BOOF! BOOF! BOOF!

Christmas Pudding attack! Argh!

What are you going to do?

I'll use the tennis racket to hit the puddings back where they came from. Turn to page 96.

I'll wave Karen's white scarf to let them know we come in peace. Turn to page 72.

"Not to worry," smiles Mrs Claus, "you've still returned Santa's lucky drawers and saved Christmas. Now, close your eyes and count to ten – I've got a surprise for you."

When you reopen your eyes, you find yourself back in your living-room. Your dad's snow-globe is still on the mantlepiece and Mrs Claus is waving at you from inside it.

"*Shake the dome,*" she mouths through the glass.

Confused, you pick up the globe and turn it over in your hands. You watch as the glitter swirls gently inside, until suddenly, looking out through your living-room window, you realise it's starting to snow.

"It's going to be a white Christmas!" you cheer, as your StoryQuest comes to a happy end. "And it's all thanks to Santa's lucky drawers."

Congratulations on completing your quest – you're a Christmas StoryQuest hero! Take a look in the back of this book for more StoryQuest adventures.

You dash towards the nearest wave and take cover from the flying ice-cubes.

"You have no idea how hot it is to run in all this fur," puffs Karen, as she slides in next to you. "I could really use a drink right now." Her eyes fix on the frozen wave. "Oo, ice – even better!"

Before you can stop her, Karen licks the frozen wave. Her long tongue sticks to its surface like glue.

"Oh, Karen, not again," sighs Hetty. "That's the fourth time this week."

Hetty has to travel all the way back to the cave to bring Karen a warm cup of tea. She uses it to thaw out her sister's tongue, by which time Santa's lucky drawers have blown miles across the Frozen Ocean.

You're *so* close to finishing your challenge, StoryQuester! Go back to make a different choice and you'll soon have those underpants back where they belong.

Go back to the start of the book to try again, or turn to page 83 to make a different choice.

Whilst King Paulus is distracted, you sneak away to a second staircase.

This one leads up to the top of the turret. From the highest step, you see the flagpole and Santa's lucky drawers still waving around in the breeze. But before you can get there, the underpants sparkle like fairy lights and take to the sky once again.

That was weird.

You're watching the drawers twirl madly around in the air, when you hear a growl from lower down in the turret. There's a large grate on the other side of the floor. It has a silver padlock and it looks like a dungeon of some sort.

Suddenly, a frosty cloud blasts out through the metal bars. Crikey, that could've frozen you solid! Do you want to find out what's growling, or will you go back to the Yeti Sisters and tell them what happened to Santa's drawers?

I'll go back to the Yeti Sisters please. Turn to page 85.

Let's take a look in the grate. Turn to page 61.

Taking Hetty's advice, you start your journey to the peak of Craggy Mountain.

It's a long and tiring walk, and when you reach the top an old troll appears from the other side of the mountain. He's green and warty, and he's pulling a wooden crate.

"What're you lot doin' up 'ere in this weather?" he asks, as an icy wind almost pushes you back down the side of the mountain. "You've gotta be a snowflake short of a blizzard to be climbin' up 'ere durin' windy season."

"Actually, we're on a very important quest," replies Letty, a little shirtily. "And we could ask you the same question – why should *you* be up here and not *us*?"

"The name's Noel the Troll," he replies. "I'm deliverin' this crate of chocolate Santas to the grotto and there's a reason only trolls are allowed on the peak of Craggy Mountain during windy season."

At the sound of his words, a huge gust of wind sweeps across the top of the mountain. Noel the Troll stands still like a statue. Or at least you *think* he's standing still like a statue, but then you realise he actually *is* a statue.

You see, trolls can turn into stone, which is how they climb mountains during the windy season.

But sadly, you're not a troll and if you don't do something, the wind will blow you and the yetis back down the side of Craggy Mountain.

I'll shelter from the wind behind the troll's crate. Turn to page 49.

I'll lie flat on my stomach so the wind can't blow me away. Turn to page 74.

"Listen up, fairies," you say, in your sternest voice, "those underpants don't belong to you, they belong to Santa, and I'm taking them back *right now*."

You take hold of the drawers and pull. Wowsers, fairies are strong! It's like trying to snatch a honey-pot off a bear.

"Mee meep-meep mee mee-meep!" cries one of them. "Mee mee-mee meep – *MEEEEEEP!*" and at once the whole flock swarms around you.

The fairies pick you up by the ears and carry you to the top of a nearby fir tree, where they sit you on the highest branch before flying away with the underpants.

Go back to the start of the book to try again, or turn to page 47 to make a different choice.

You step out onto the Frozen Ocean. Wow, it's slippery, but sliding down the icy waves is also kind of fun.

Suddenly, an ice-cube flies in out of nowhere. It whistles past your ear, hits the frozen wave behind you and smashes like glass, as another shoots over your head.

"It's Jack Frost!" wails Letty. "He's pummelling us with ice-cubes! I thought Christmas puddings were bad enough, but at least they were soft. What are we going to do?"

"We could make slushies with them," shrugs Karen.

You can't follow Karen's suggestion, because, well, it's a stupid one. Which means you have two choices: hit the ice-cubes back with the tennis racket, or take cover behind one of the frozen waves.

To take cover behind a wave, turn to page 52.

To hit the ice-cubes with the racket, turn to page 63.

Brandishing your tennis racket like a pro-player, you thwack the Christmas puddings back towards the castle.

The head of a walrus pops up on the highest turret. One of the puddings hits him right between the eyes. It explodes in a jumble of currants and cherries.

The walrus wipes his face with the back of his flipper, and, "LOAD THE CATAPULT!" he bawls.

A group of wooden soldiers wheel an enormous catapult onto the roof. They place something wobbly into the sling. You can't make out what it is, but it's roughly the size of an elephant and…is that *cream* on top of it?

"It's a giant strawberry trifle!" yells Betty. "Quick, everyone, take cover!"

The catapult flings the gigantic dessert across the wall of the castle, where it lands on top of you with a loud—

SPLAT!

The world goes dark and sticky, but it tastes fantastic. It's going to take forever to eat your way out of here and frankly you couldn't care less.

Scrummy!

Go back to the start of the book to try again, or turn to page 87 to make a different choice.

StoryQuest

CHOOSE THE PAGE - UNLOCK THE ADVENTURE

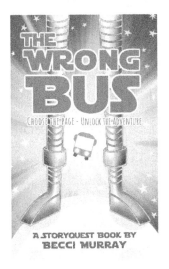

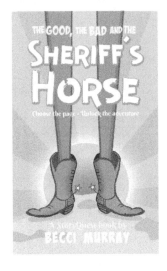

Have you tried these other StoryQuest adventure
books? Available now in paperback or eBook.

Laugh along with Billy, as he boosts his brain to the size of Venus in this hilarious five-star chapter book also by Becci Murray.

Or try these very serious poems about really important stuff (like sausages, yaks and toenails) in this illustrated collection of rhyming silliness.

Becci Murray is a British author from Gloucestershire. She used to run a children's entertainment company, where she earned a living playing musical bumps and doing the Hokey Cokey (true story). Her favourite books are by Roald Dahl and she has a life-size BFG sticker on her bedroom wall (well, almost life-size).

You can learn more about Becci or send her a message by visiting the Llama House Children's Books website – she would love to hear from you!

www.llamahousebooks.com

Made in the USA
Middletown, DE
12 December 2020